I'm Gonna Tell Mama I Want An Iguana

poems by TONY JOHNSTON

illustrated by LILLIAN HOBAN

G. P. PUTNAM'S SONS   NEW YORK

For Myra Cohn Livingston
and
Arthur Levine
—TJ

Text copyright © 1990 by Tony Johnston
Illustrations copyright © 1990 by Lillian Hoban
All rights reserved. This book, or parts thereof, may not be reproduced
in any form without permission in writing from the publisher.
G.P. Putnam's Sons, a division of The Putnam & Grosset Group,
200 Madison Avenue, New York, NY 10016.
Published simultaneously in Canada.
Printed in Hong Kong by South China Printing Co. (1988) Ltd.
Library of Congress Cataloging-in-Publication Data
Johnston, Tony. I'm gonna tell Mama I want an iguana.
Summary: An illustrated collection of twenty-three
humorous poems on a variety of subjects.
1. Children's poetry, American. [1. Humorous poetry.
2. American poetry] I. Hoban, Lillian, ill. II. Title.
PS3560.039314 1990 811'.54 88-32397
ISBN 0-339-21934-X
1 3 5 7 9 10 8 6 4 2
First impression

LIST OF POEMS

LIZARD LONGING

For Sam and for Tim Takeuchi

I'm gonna tell Mama
I want an iguana,
all blinky and scaly
just like a piranha.
I don't want some flora,
I'd rather have fauna.
I'm gonna tell Mama
I want an iguana.

BAD DECISION

A bull saw something red.
He gored it.
It was a fire engine.
He should have
ignored it.

BOING!

Grasshopper
leaping
on the lawn.
   Hop,
      hop
like popcorn.
He's enjoying
where he's going.
Boing!

FROG EGGS

Frog eggs.
Jelly dots
all sopping.

One day
they'll do lots
of hopping.

SKELETON TRAIN

Clackety-clack goes the skeleton train.
Clackety-clack down the skeleton track.
Rattlety-rat plays the skeleton band.
All aboard, please! moans the bony trainman.
Tickety-tick clicks the tickety taker.
Boo-ity-boo! shouts the skeleton crew.
Whoo-ity-whooo! wails the whistle inside.
Bye-ity-bye! wave the ones who don't ride.
Then
Clackety-clack goes the skeleton train.
Clackety-clack down the skeleton track.
WHOOOOOOOOOOOOO
knows if it ever comes bickety-back?

UPSIDE-DOWNER

I'd like to skibble softly up the walls,
to shoot and scoot and scamper over ceilings,
to scout for bugs from threads hung in the halls,
and then I'd know an upside-downer's feelings.

SAD POTATOES

Potatoes have a lot of little eyes.
So
do they cry a lot of little cries?

AT THE ZOO

The crocodiles stare.
They never blink.
They lie there
in their log jam in the sun.
and doze.

Maybe they think
of swimming
free somewhere.
One has a penny on
its nose.

AMONG THE WATER LILIES

A fat frog lurking
among the water lilies.
He slurps. Then he burps.

DOG BISCUITS

For Ashley

There are dog biscuits in
a big box
on the shelf.
Little cookie bones I'd
like to taste
for myself.

So I wiggle the box,
and I jiggle
out three.
I feed one to my dog,
and I feed
two to me.

VISITING THE VET

My dog is trembling
in the car.
He feels where we are going.
My dog is huddled
by the door,
worn out with all that knowing.
So I am whispering in his ear,
"I am here, boy, I am here."

OVERDOG

Overdog Johnson is a guy
who always wins
but hardly tries.

Pitcher sails it.
Johnson nails it.
Whack!
Home run!

Pitcher steams it.
Johnson creams it.
Thwack!
Home run!

Pitcher smokes it.
Johnson pokes it.
Smack!
Home run!

Pitcher fires it.
Johnson wires it.
Crack!
Ho-hum.

A LITTLE CHRISTMAS TREE

I stand outside
and snow comes down,
quietly down on me.
And soon I am
all quietly white,
a little Christmas tree,
standing so still
on a little hill
somewhere
under the stars.

WHICH SHOES TO CHOOSE?

If I were a spider,
now that would be fine.
I'd use all my shoes at
the very same time!

BEACH ROSE

For Jenny

I am walking on the shore.
The foam flies.
The rain falls.
The wind blows.
My umbrella opens like
a red rose.

A LITTLE SEED

How I would like to be a little seed!
(A daisy or a pansy or a weed.)
And have the fun of hearing someone shout,
"*Oh, look! Here's Spring!*"
When I come popping out.

TO GROW ON

Sooooooooooosh.
Just like a balloon
I swell up and grow
when I suck my breath in slow.

WHOOOOOOOOOOOSH!
The air rushes out
in a beautiful blow—
and there my candles go!

WINDSTORM IN BROOKLYN

Brooklyn was swept by a
windstorm one day.
Afghans and poodles were
carried away.
Children slurped cereal,
soaring aloft.
Some of them bumped into
clouds (pillow-soft).
Ladies with teacups sipped
tea on the fly.
Criss-crossing neighbors yelled,
"Hi!" in the sky.
Most of the city was
tossed in the air—
except for the birds, which were
already there.

AERIAL SHEET MUSIC

Black birds
Sitting on the telephone
Wires
Look like notes
So fat.
　　　Then—
They all stand up,
They clear
Their throats,
And sing the song
They sat.

JELLYFISH WALK

When jellyfish go walking,
there isn't any talking
or giggling.
There's *phlup, phlup, phlup.*

When jellyfish are stopping,
there's plenty of slip-slopping
and jiggling
to stop, stop, stop.

ONCE UPON A TIME

Grandma is Grandma.
Her hair
is always up.
Twisted, knotted,
anchored with pins
to hold it there.

Once upon a time
I saw it falling down,
a silver riverspill.
She was Rapunzel.

SUNSET

Day took the pennies
from her pocket,
melted them all,
and poured them
over the hills.

NIGHT LIGHT

A star fell down from far away.
I picked it up from where it lay
in sparkling dust and took it home
across the fields as night came on.

Beside my bed I placed it, then.
It twinkled back to life again,
and gave off such a lovely light
I wasn't scared of dark all night.